W9-AMM-715

To my sweet Audrey,
who continues to leave her mark
on every page of the story . . .

Learn more about Angie at AngieSmithOnline.com. To read more about the baby that inspired this story, read Angie's book, *I Will Carry You* (978-0-8054-6428-3).

copyright © 2013 by Angie Smith, Nashville, Tennessee
Published in 2013 by B&H Publishing Group, Nashville, Tennessee
ISBN: 978-1-4336-8045-8

Dewey Decimal Classification: JF
Subject Heading: LOVE–FICTION \ RABBITS–FICTION \ SELF-ESTEEM–FICTION

Scripture reference taken from the Holman ChristianStandard Bible® (HCSB),
copyright © 1999, 2000, 2002, 2003, by Holman Bible Publishers.
Also used: English Standard Bible (ESV), copyright © 2001 by Crossway Bibles,
a publishing ministry of Good News Publishers.

All rights reserved. Printed in Malaysia.
October 2018
4 5 6 7 8 9 10 • 22 21 20 19 18

Audrey Bunny

a story by
Angie Smith

with illustrations by
Breezy Brookshire

KIDS
Nashville, Tennessee

The little bunny looked up from the bottom of the big, dark barrel. She wondered if she would ever be chosen. Months had passed as Bunny waited and watched, watched and waited. She was once one of twelve bunnies, but now there were only two.

A few days earlier, a little girl had come to the shop, and Bunny had tried as hard as she could to look perfect. For a moment, the little girl had looked right at her and even said something to her mother. But the bunny couldn't understand.

Then the little girl left. And the bunny knew why.

Bunny wasn't like the others. She had a smudge right over her heart. What little girl would want a messed-up toy? The mark had been there for as long as Bunny could remember, and she knew it wouldn't come off. Other children had tried to remove it. When they saw that they couldn't, they set her back down and chose another toy.

What happened to bunnies that were never chosen?
Did they live in the barrel forever?

Just then, the shop's door chime rang.

"Hello, may I help you?" the shopkeeper asked.

"Yes ma'am. Today is my birthday, and I'm here to choose a toy. May I take a look?"

"Of course." She pointed to where Bunny and the other toys were located.

Bunny peeked over the animals in the barrel.

It was her! It was the same little girl from a few days ago.

She straightened her ears as high as they would go and
squeezed her eyes shut as the little girl walked in her direction.
She was too nervous to look.

Could today be the day she got picked?

She felt the girl's warm hands touch her ears. Then she remembered: her mark. She couldn't let the little girl see that she was a messed-up, not-so-perfect bunny.

As Bunny was lifted out of the barrel, she let her arm fall just so it covered the mark over her heart.

"This is the one! This is the bunny I want for my birthday." She hugged the bunny to her chest, and Bunny loved her right away. "May I have her, Mother?" Her mother nodded.

"Oh, what shall I name you? Or do you prefer Bunny?" Caroline giggled.

Bunny considered the question. She never dreamed she would have a real name.

"I know! I will call you Audrey. It was my grandma's name, and I've always thought it was perfect. *Audrey Bunny.*"

Bunny felt her heart warm as she looked over Caroline's shoulder. If she could only keep her mark hidden, Caroline might actually believe *she* was perfect too.

That night, when it was time for stories and warm milk,
Caroline hugged Audrey tight and tucked her into the covers.
As soon as Caroline went to brush her teeth, Audrey pulled
them up just a little higher to cover her mark.

12

When the lights went out, Caroline smiled.
"I love you, Audrey Bunny."
Oh, *sweet Caroline*, Audrey thought, *I love you too*.

"Wake up, Caroline," Mother called. "Today we are going to the lake!"

"Oh, Audrey. You will love the lake! We will have to find you a beautiful swimsuit." Caroline smiled and ran to change.

Oh no! My mark! Audrey thought.

"Well, you silly thing!" Caroline exclaimed when she came back. "How did you manage that?" She bent low and scooped up Audrey, kissing her as she tucked her in the bag.

Audrey's secret was safe for today.

Caroline made Audrey feel like she was alive. Every day, after Caroline left, Audrey would watch through the window until the big yellow bus stopped out front again. She felt her heart get warmer as the footsteps came closer, up the stairs, until the doorknob turned.

Then, they would play.

Sometimes they had tea. Some days they read books. Sometimes they played dress-up. They could be nurses, ballerinas, or adventurers. But it was always the two of them, and Audrey was happier than she ever thought she could be.

"I love you, Audrey Bunny," Caroline whispered.

And I love you, sweet Caroline, Audrey thought.

One afternoon, Caroline
propped Audrey up on her bed
and smiled big.

"Tomorrow will be a special day,"
Caroline whispered to her. "You won't stay
home with Mother. You will go to school with
me and meet my friends." Audrey listened.

"It's called Show and Tell." Caroline rubbed
Audrey's bunny ears.

Audrey had never met Caroline's friends before,
and it might be exciting to ride in the big, yellow
bus and go to a new place. She wanted to make
Caroline proud.

That night, while Caroline slept, Audrey
watched the moon and thought about
how her life had changed. It was too
wonderful for words.

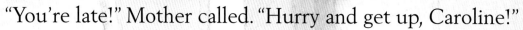

"You're late!" Mother called. "Hurry and get up, Caroline!"

"OH! Oh dear!" Caroline jumped out of bed and scrambled to find her clothes. She ran to the bathroom and brushed out a few tangles before her mother called again.

"Caroline, the bus is coming!"

Audrey sadly watched Caroline jump down the hallway while trying to put on her shoe. It was Show and Tell day, and Caroline had forgotten her. She wanted to call out the window to stop the big yellow bus. But she didn't see Caroline.

Suddenly, Audrey heard footsteps again, running up the stairs, down the hallway, and there she was. Caroline pulled Audrey from the covers and held her close. For a moment, Audrey felt relief. But it didn't last long.

As Caroline tucked Audrey in her backpack, she remembered: *My mark! There is nothing to cover my mark!*

Audrey watched the house get smaller and smaller as
Caroline walked down the sidewalk and up the big bus stairs.
Caroline took her seat beside a bubbly little girl. "Not until we get
to Show and Tell," Caroline said, closing the zipper on her backpack.
The little girl giggled with excitement, but Audrey began to cry.

Audrey wiped at the smudge. Why couldn't she be perfect? It was only a matter of time before Caroline saw her mark and returned her to the store.

"I love you, sweet Caroline," she whispered to the dark.

"This is my Audrey Bunny." With warm hands around her ears, Audrey was pulled high in the air. It reminded Audrey of her first day with Caroline, those hands lifting her out.

The kids were all staring at her.

"I see it!" a boy in the back exclaimed.

"I do too!" said another.

"May we look closely?" a little girl asked.

The teacher nodded, and they all gathered around Audrey, taking turns touching her mark.

The mark. Oh, it was too terrible to be real. . . .

She would always love her Caroline, even from the bottom of that deep, dark barrel.

"So your mother told you that if she was meant to be yours, she would still be there?" another girl asked, running her finger along the mark.

"Yes. And as soon as I saw her, I knew that she was my bunny."

Oh, Caroline. If only you knew!

Slowly and as tenderly as that first day, Caroline looked right into Audrey's eyes. Then she lifted up her bunny ear and whispered, "I've always known, Audrey Bunny. The spot over your heart made you beautiful to me." Caroline's eyes glistened as she finished. "I chose you, Audrey, and I love you more than you could ever know."

Audrey stared at Caroline and tried to take in her words.
She didn't need the bandages or silly clothes to hide the mark.
Those hands . . . they had known all the while.

It wasn't a secret she had to keep.

It was the reason she was chosen to begin with.

As the children finally made their way back to their seats, Audrey sat up taller than she ever had before. There would be no going back to the barrel, no more tears, and no more hiding what made her different. Caroline loved her, just as she was.

Audrey smiled and rested her head on Caroline's shoulder.

And I love you, my sweet Caroline.

I praise you, for I am fearfully and wonderfully made.
Wonderful are your works; my soul knows it very well.
—Psalm 139:14 (ESV)

Remember:

Your hands made me and formed me. —Psalm 119:73 (HCSB)

Read:

Read Psalm 119:73. Did you know that God created you, even from the very beginning of your life? He even knows how many hairs are on your head (Matthew 10:30)! Isn't that amazing? There's nothing about you that happened by chance; He designed you in His image and He loves you!

Think:

1. Why does Audrey Bunny think her smudge is bad?
2. Is there something about you that you don't like?
3. How does Caroline change how Audrey Bunny feels about herself?
4. How does God see you?
5. Does that change how you feel about yourself?

Do:

Write a letter to yourself—from God.

1. Ask an adult for some nice stationery (paper with matching envelope) or make your own!
2. Read Psalm 119:73 above and read Genesis 1.
3. Think about what God says about you, about how He made you.
4. At the top of the paper, write "Dear" and your name. Now, fill that paper with what God thinks of you, what God says about you in His Word.
5. Put the letter in a special place. When you're feeling not-so-perfect, take it out and read it. Read it until you believe every word.

It's true. God loves you and created you just the way you are.